Planet Odd

'Planet Odd'
An original concept by Jenny Jinks
© Jenny Jinks

Illustrated by Román Diaz

Published by MAVERICK ARTS PUBLISHING LTD

Studio 11, City Business Centre, 6 Brighton Road,

Horsham, West Sussex, RH13 5BB

© Maverick Arts Publishing Limited February 2020

+44 (0)1403 256941

A CIP catalogue record for this book is available at the British Library.

ISBN 978-1-84886-656-0

www.maverickbooks.co.uk

Yellow

This book is rated as: Yellow Band (Guided Reading)
This story is mostly decodable at Letters and Sounds Phase 3.
Up to eight non-decodable story words are included.

Planet Odd

by **Jenny Jinks**

illustrated by
Román Diaz

Kip was in his rocket.

CRASH!

"This planet is odd," said Kip.

"It is red."

Kip did not like odd things.

Kip met Zak.

"This planet is odd," said Kip.

"You look different to me."

Zak smiled at Kip.

11

Zak got a ball.

"This planet is odd," said Kip.

"The ball is odd, too!"

Zak hit the ball to Kip.

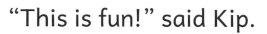

"This is fun!" said Kip.

The ball seems OK.

"Get in my car," said Zak.

"This planet is odd," said Kip.

"This car is odd too!"

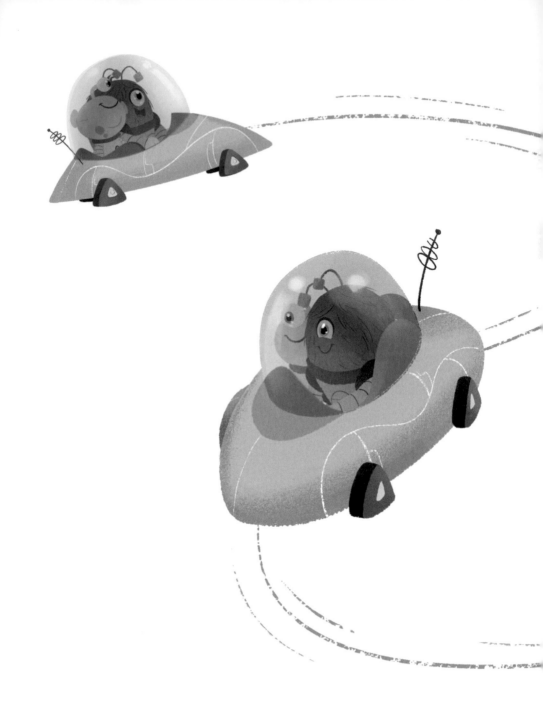

"Wheeeee!" said Kip.

The car seems OK...

Zak looked at Kip's rocket.

"I can fix it!" he said.

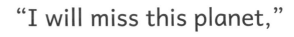

"I will miss this planet," said Kip.

"I will miss you," said Zak.

"Get in my rocket," said Kip.

Zoom!

"This planet is odd," said Zak.

"Yes," said Kip.

He looked at his planet.

"But it is home."

Quiz

1. What colour is Zak's planet?
a) Green
b) Red
c) Yellow

2. The ball is...
a) Odd
b) Silly
c) Small

3. What did Zak do to Kip's rocket?
a) Fix it
b) Break it
c) Fly it

4. "Get in my _____," said Kip.
a) Boat
b) Ship
c) Rocket

5. What colour is Kip's planet?
a) Purple
b) Blue
c) Pink

Book Bands for Guided Reading

The Institute of Education book banding system is a scale of colours that reflects the various levels of reading difficulty. The bands are assigned by taking into account the content, the language style, the layout and phonics. Word, phrase and sentence level work is also taken into consideration.

Maverick Early Readers are a bright, attractive range of books covering the pink to white bands. All of these books have been book banded for guided reading to the industry standard and edited by a leading educational consultant.

Pink
Red
Yellow
Blue
Green
Orange
Turquoise
Purple
Gold
White

To view the whole Maverick Readers scheme, visit our website at

www.maverickearlyreaders.com

Or scan the QR code above to view our scheme instantly!

Quiz Answers: 1b, 2a, 3a, 4c, 5b